W9-CAT-224

123 SESAME STREET

A Wish for Grover

By Allison Davis
Adapted by Shawn Currie
Illustrated by Tom Brannon
Grover performed by Eric Jacobson

publications international, ltd.

Play-a-Story™ Animated Storybook

Sometimes at bedtime, if I am not sleepy, do you know what I do? I look out my window and imagine. Oh, look! The first star in the sky—and it is a *shooting* star!

What should I wish for tonight...?

...To soar to the moon in a rocket ship? But I, Grover, get airsick in rockets.

...To have super powers?
I already have super powers.

...To live in a faraway jungle? I have never lived in a faraway jungle before. Yes! I, Grover, will wish to live in a faraway jungle.

What if my wish came true? Imagine...

In the jungle, I have my own tree house. Climb up and I will show you around.

Elmo lives in the very next tree, so there is another cute, furry monster to keep me company...because it is more fun when a monster has a friend.

But some days, I am happy just being on my own with the fuzzy and feathery little animals.

Hello there, pretty parrot.
All kinds of jungle friends come to visit. I, Grover, have the most popular tree house in all the jungle. What can I say? I am a happening monster.

From my lookout post high up in the tip-top of a tree, I can see all the way to the sea.

I use my trusty spyglass to keep a close watch for pirates...or should I say parrots?

Yes siree, I am a master jungle watcher. Nothing gets past Jungle Grover.

Polly want a coconut?

Whether searching for pirates or parrots, you can be sure that I, Grover, am watching over the jungle day and night to make sure all is well.

Okay, so mostly over the day. A monster needs his sleep, you know.

You can see that my tree house kitchen has lots of yummy fruit. That is so I can share bananas, mangoes, dates, and all kinds of tasty treats with my friends.

WAIT A MINUTE!

Dates? *Dates*? Who put that on the shopping list? Oh, well...

Dates on spikelet

Cross section of a date fruit

epicarp (skin)

perianth

endocarp

mesocarp (flesh)

seed

If a guest ever gets thirsty, here is a handy little maneuver. I put my cute little cup outside this window and catch water from a waterfall.

But my favorite jungle drink is fresh coconut milk. I like to share a coconut with a monkey friend of mine. A very *strong* monkey friend of mine. How refreshing!

All day long, jungle neighbors drop in to play with Elmo and me. We play games like Monkey See, Monkey Do. I am quite the expert at this game. But...come closer so I may whisper this in your ear...but I must keep an eye on the other players. They like to get into monkey business.

Sometimes I, Grover, find the time to play Follow the Leader. Swinging from vines is the best way to get around the jungle.

Catch me if you can!

aaa aah!

Oh. I, Grover of the Jungle, forgot to watch out for the jungle trees.

Vines may be the best way around the jungle, but they are not the safest.

When things get muddy, the jungle is an easy place to find a bath. All you need is a pool of water, a bristly brush, and a first-rate scrubber-monkey.

Oh. That's good...a little down and to the left...that's it!

Oh, and do you know the best jungle game of all? Hide-and-Seek! There are so many sneaky places to hide in the jungle.

Ready or not, here I come!

The hiders do not fool me. I know furry friends are hiding all around. Wait a minute. Did I just see something furry in a big tree? I am sure I heard something rustle in the leafy bushes.
Oh, little lion...oh, little monkey...oh, everybody... come out, come out, wherever you are!

Oh my goodness, it is getting dark now. It is time to go home to bed. All the animal mommies are picking up their babies.

That is strange. I do not see my mommy anywhere.

Mommy?

Mommy!

Mommy!

MOMMY!

Oh, there she is. Just when I need her. Just like always.

"Oh, Mommy!" I say. "I missed you! I do not wish to live far away in a jungle. Even for all the coconuts in the world." My mommy looks a little surprised. I do not blame her. It has been a strange night.

NEW WISH

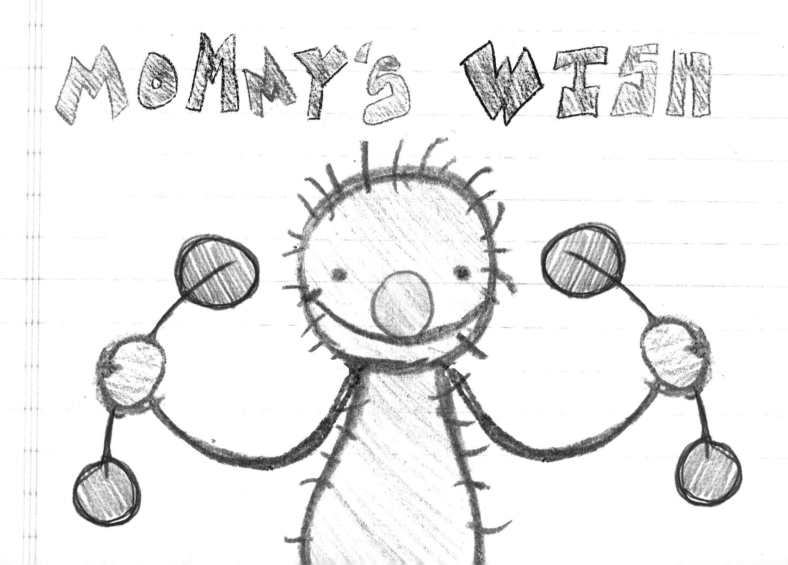

I hug my mommy and tell her that I want to change my wish. My new wish is that my mommy would tuck me into bed.

And then she whispers, "And *I* wish *you* would go to sleep so you will grow up big and furry and strong."

MOMMY'S WISH